A Dead Politician,
An Undead Clam,
And An Ancient Horror

Three Rhode Island Nightmares

by Mark Binder

Light Publications
Providence

Also by Mark Binder
Fictions
What Cheer
The Groston Rules
A Dead Politician, an Undead Clam,
and an Ancient Horror
Loki Ragnarok
It Ate My Sister
The Zombie Cat
The Rationalization Diet

Stories for young people
Cinderella Spinderella
The Bed Time Story Book
Kings, Wolves, Princesses and Lions
Genies, Giants and a Walrus
Classic Stories for Boys and Girls
Tall Tales, Whoppers and Lies
It was a dark and stormy night…
Stories for Peace
Transmit Joy!

as Izzy Abrahmson
The Village Life Series
A Village Romance
Winter Blessings
The Village Feasts
The Village Twins
The Council of Wise Women (Soon…)

The Vampire Clams of Narragansett Bay

Local Shellfishman Mystery Closed

Beloved clammer William "Bivalve Bill" Peterson was declared legally dead today, after vanishing mysteriously seven years ago.

"He went out one morning with his bull rake and he never came back," said his wife, Martha Peterson, "I miss him terribly."

A well-known expert on the history of clamming, Peterson was frequently interviewed by national television and media outlets. At the time of his disappearance, Peterson was 79. Police believe he became disoriented and drowned.

"That's nonsense," said Daniel Duggan,

also a professional shellfisher. "Bill was healthy, never missed a day's clamming. It were the clams that done him in."
– from *The Narragansett Times*

Early Halloween morning before the sun's up isn't a time most people spend standing in salt water up to their elbows. Narragansett Bay can be mighty cold, and the slightest breeze feels like the icy finger of winter to come.

Daniel Duggan didn't mind. Not much anyway. Even though the sky was dark, the full moon was high and the tide was nice and low.

As his father had told him, "Some peoples say you gotta make hay when the sun shines. I say, we gotta dig clams when the water's right."

The corner of Dan's mouth twitched at the memory. Pa used to call landfolk "peoples," like they were pimples. Pa had been dead more than sixty years, and his voice was still clear. Clearer than most stuff in Dan's head.

Dan leaned down and dragged his rake back, listening and feeling for the scrape that said he'd gotten a few clams. You could hear them, if you listened hard enough. Hear them underwater. Feel them up the length of the ash rake handle. And they whistle sometimes when they're in the cooler.

There weren't many clammers left who knew such. Summers the ranks swelled, and the price of a littleneck dropped to near nothing. It was after Labor Day that the real professionals showed their worth. Alarms set to the tide's schedule. Equipment always loaded in the truck. Coffee in a thermos. Waders hanging over the hook on the back door where they'd dripped and dried the night before. Some of the new kids wore wet suits and dry suits. Didn't know about wool underwear. Heavy but warm. Kept you centered and down, like a rock so you didn't get pulled this way and that by the tide.

Fewer real clammers anymore. No one retired from digging clams, you just died. It was something that landfolk didn't understand. The water kept you young. The work kept you strong and limber. The exhaustion and determination to pull a living from the salt kept you alive. Clammers died in their beds, not out in the waves.

And they didn't just vanish.

Except four more had gone missing over the last few years. One down in Watch Hill, two in South County and one in East Greenwich.

Like something was moving up the Bay.

Dan heard the scrape, and pulled up the rake. He fished through the basket and fingered a dozen littlenecks, two cherrystones and a chowder along with three smaller-than-legal seed clams and a whelk. Some folk were collecting the whelks, selling them to Portuguese and Italian restaurants, but Dan still didn't like them. They ate clams, ruined his livelihood. He frowned, and dropped the big snail into the floating bushel basket tied to a rope attached to his suspenders. No harm in pulling the big snails out. Get enough, maybe make a few dollars.

He threw the seeds back, flipped the rake over, shook out its teeth, and dug in.

"Diggah Dan." That's what they called him behind his back, mocking him for what he did. Made him smile a little. Little pissants who had no idea how to work and wouldn't know a callus from a tumor. Thought he'd be too thin skinned to hear them say it to his face? What the hell did they know.

Dan leaned into the rake and began backing up slowly.

That's when he felt it. Something sharp cutting into his right foot. Through the waders, cold water immediately flooding into rubber boots, through the thick sole and leather of his work boot, and through his wool sock.

Sharp sudden pain that went away almost instantly. Gone.

Didn't feel the cold water in the waders. Didn't feel the ache of his knees.

What the hell?

Numbness. Sumpthin.

Dan frowned.

Peoples believed that clammers were slow. Thought, truth be told, that they were retarded. Doing something mindless day after day, hour after hour in the cold dark, wet, hot. Didn't matter what day, what season. There were clams, and the clammers dug them. Peoples didn't seem to realize that their Spaghetti Alle Vongole had to come from somewhere. From someone.

Reality was that clammers had lots of time for thinking and just doing. Shallow waters, deep thoughts. Dan had once met the Dalai Lama, purely by accident at a rest stop on I-95. Not every day you see a guy in an orange robe standing next one over at the urinal. Can't help but wonder how you pee in those robes… After they finished and washed their hands, Dan and the Dalai Lama had given each other the once over, smiled and nodded. Recognized their similarities. No words necessary.

Just two guys doing their thing and being.

Probably Dan had just stepped on some summer asshole's lost clam rake. One of the big sharp teeth had punctured up into his foot. But that didn't explain the rapid sensation that the entire world was going away into darkness.

Dan realized that he was drifting and lurching. Rather than wait for the water in the waders to come up to his ass, he dropped his rake—never done that even in the middle of a hurricane—took a breath, balanced on his left leg, bent down, took another breath, head under water, felt around the edge of his heel, and found it. Something.

It was attached.

Jesus. His heart nearly stopped.

The Narragansetts had a story about the death from under the sand. It was said that they were an ancient evil created to balance the good of the harvest. Man took from the sea, and the sea took back. The Indians called it the *sucki poquauhock*, which had always made Dan and the other clammers laugh. Poquauhock was a clam of course, but sucki sounded a lot like sucky, which was what clams did when they filtered the waters of the bay. In Narragansett though, sucki meant black. The black clam. The death clam. And nobody, none of the whites anyway, believed that such a thing could exist.

Dan's mouth and ear were under water as he reached down. His fingers were going numb, even as he felt the round hard thing attached to his heel.

He bit his tongue hard to stay focused, grabbed on to whatever it was, and pulled.

It came off easy. Easier than he'd imagined it would. He'd imagined effort, like opening a bear trap or getting a biting dog to let go. But it wasn't difficult. Just slid off.

The moment it came loose the pain shot up his leg like he'd been stabbed with a razor. He nearly fell over, nearly passed out.

Dan wobbled and set his inflamed right foot back down on the bottom. He winced and lifted his head out of the frigid bay, gasping for breath even though he hadn't held it for more than a moment.

The sun was just coming up, bright red and purple and beautiful and orange.

He held up his right hand and looked at the thing.

It was big, the size of a black dessert plate, and dark as the night without moon or stars—except for the sharp bloody white spike that stuck straight out between its twin shells.

It was pulsing in Dan's hand, wriggling and squirming, more like a squid or a fish than any clam Dan had ever met.

It seemed to be thinking. It seemed to be hunting. As he stared at it, it was opening and closing. The spike was darting in and out, one inch, two inches, three inches, four, aiming for Dan's head like it had eyes and wanted to kill him.

The thing was rolling in Dan's hand, trying to break free. It felt like there was a gyroscope inside it.

Tugging and twirling and stabbing. Stabbing. He lifted it up, bringing it closer and closer to his face.

Dan felt some of the poison still moving in his blood, slowing his thoughts.

It was staring at him. It was inside him. It was hungry.

Dan held it in both hands, level with his eyes, watching the soft inside of the clam quiver, the sharp spike vibrate.

For one absurd moment he felt like he wanted to kiss it. It was something like passion, this desire to bring the clam to his mouth and press it to his lips, to taste its saltiness, even though he knew that the fang would puncture his tongue and skewer his jaw, crawl into his throat and suck him dry.

If a bright gleam of a white sunray hadn't glinted off the gray water of the bay into his eyes, Dan might have kissed that clam.

But the light made him blink, and the blink broke the spell, and with a primal groan of "NO!" Dan lifted the sucki poquauhock high over his head and hurled it out as far as he could, deep and away from the sand where he stood.

He stood for a moment, heart racing, eyes blinking, water dripping from his hair and ears. Fingers clenched tightly as if they still held it. Panting. Cold.

Alive.

Dan took a deep breath. Then another. Then he nodded. No point in standing around waiting to freeze.

He took a few more breaths, then held his, knelt down, felt around and found the handle of his rake where he'd dropped it. Not going to lose a tool. Have to buy a new one. Not going to leave it to rust or injure someone like a summer asshole. Hell with that.

He stood up, rake in right hand, blinked the stinging salt water from his eyes. He lifted the rake high up into the air, held it horizontal for a moment, and shook it at the sun.

Thanks, he thought. Then he smiled, embarrassed.

Dan glanced at the bushel basket floating inside its foam life preserver, only half full of clams.

Never be able to tell anyone about this. Shoulda dropped the vampire clam into the bushel. Brought it back into shore. Give it to those marine folk at University of Rhode Island. Or sell it to some billionaire gourmet looking for a thrill. Make a million. Retire. Famous.

Shoulda kept the damned thing out of the sea instead of throwing it back.

Shoulda, Dan thought. Too late. Didn't.

Enough for today?

Yeah. Given the hole in the waders and the temperature of the water. Can't say it would be a good idea to keep digging. Not today. Probably should get a tetanus booster, too.

Kissing a clam? Dan snorted. Crazy.

Time to go in. He sighed. Hated to leave without filling his bushel. Still.

He looked off at the patch of water where the thing had splashed down. Most clams don't move more than a foot or two from the place they grow. This thing? He didn't know. He could go and visit with his cousins down in Florida. They were always talking about how nice and warm it was in the winter.

Time to go in.

Dan leaned the bull rake on his shoulder, let the bushel basket float behind him, and limped back to shore.

More clams tomorrow. Always more clams tomorrow.

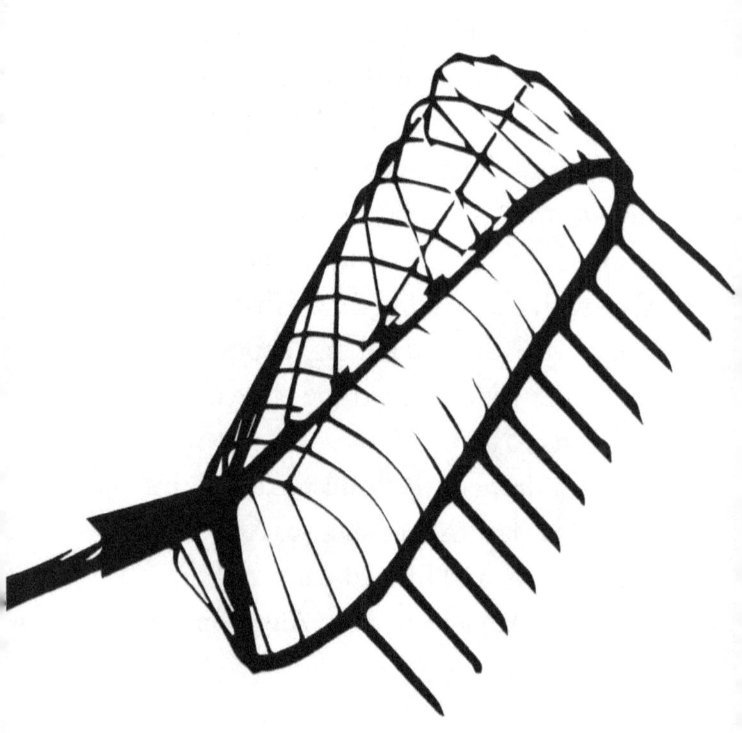

Old Scratch Nickels

based on a true story

Old Scratch Nickels was a corrupt city councilman. He would take a bribe for just about anything. If you needed a building permit or a liquor license, he was your go to guy. You could fix a zoning variance or a parking ticket with him. Just put a deposit of cash into his desk drawer and you could get anything done.

He liked to go out and eat dinner at lots of different restaurants, and he never once paid the bill. Nobody dared give him the check. At the end of the night, the owner would just walk over and say,

"It's on the house." They knew that if they tried to make him pay, the next day the building inspector, the fire inspector and the health inspector would all show up and close them down.

The restaurant that Old Scratch liked to go to best was called The Bloated Chicken.

The Bloated Chicken served all kinds of chicken. They had fried chicken, baked chicken, and broiled chicken. They had chicken wings, chicken fingers, chicken tenders and chicken nuggets. They had chicken soup, chicken a la king, chicken tetrazzini, chicken fried rice…

Old Scratch Nickels only ordered one thing, The Bloated Chicken Challenge.

The Bloated Chicken Challenge was simple. You had twenty-two minutes to eat an entire fried chicken with baked potato, mashed potatoes, cole slaw and gravy. If you did eat it in twenty-two minutes—or less—your meal was free.

Never mind the fact that he never paid for the meal, Old Scratch liked the challenge. Especially since he'd never beaten it.

One night, he came in real late, just after closing, and ordered the challenge.

The Bloated Chicken's Owner, Washington Jefferson the Third was the last one there at this point. He cooked up the meal, put it down in front of Old Scratch, and started the chess clock running.

Old Scratch Nickels was this big fat guy, and when he started to eat, it was terrible to behold. He was chewing like a maniac.

It was disgusting. Grease splattered, fat flew, bits of skin slurped into his maw. He didn't bother with fork and knife, even with the mashed potatoes and gravy.

Washington Jefferson the Third, who was sweeping up, tried to tune out the revoltingly atonal symphony of mastication, gulping and grunting.

Old Scratch was just shoving it all down at breakneck speed.

Everybody thought that the hardest part of the Bloated Chicken Challenge was baked potato, mashed potato, and the gravy. It wasn't. Nobody ever beat the challenge because that cole slaw was thick and heavy.

This night, though, Old Scratch had slurped down the slaw and was making good time.

He only had thirty-four seconds left on the clock and a little bit of meat on the wishbone.

He threw the wishbone up into

the air. He caught it in his mouth and started to cough.

The victory bell rang.

Old Scratch Nickels stood up, knocked his chair over and began to stagger. He had his hands upraised, as if in triumph.

It took Washington Jefferson the Third a moment or two to process the change from gorging to gagging. He looked at Old Scratch, and then he looked at the sign on the wall.

Old Scratch Nickels was dancing around. He was making that noise. He was pointing at his throat.

But he wasn't turning blue. No, he definitely wasn't turning blue.

Then boom, Old Scratch Nickels fell to the ground.

Washington Jefferson the Third dropped his broom, went over, knelt down and felt for a pulse. There was nothing.

"Oh my God," Washington Jefferson the Third thought. "Old Scratch Nickels is dead."

He didn't know what to do.

"They're going to think I killed him on purpose. They're going to put me into the electric chair and fry me for sure."

Then he remembered, there was a dumpster out back. Trash collection was the next afternoon.

He grabbed Old Scratch Nickels by the ankles, man he was heavy, and dragged him out the back door, down the alley, and into the dumpster. He put a piece of cardboard over the body, shut the dumpster door, went back to the restaurant and washed the dishes, scoured the floor with bleach, erased the videotapes, locked up, went home, and slept very soundly.

Well, later that night, stumbling back to his favorite resting place, was Homeless Hal.

Homeless Hal opened the door to his dumpster. He went in.

He saw somebody's feet sticking out from under a piece of cardboard.

"Hey, man," Hal muttered. "What'cho doin' there? This is my spot."

The guy didn't answer.

"Hey! Come on, get out! This is my place. I'm gonna take care of you."

Homeless Hal reached down, he picked up a board.

"Hey! I got a two-by-four. I'm going to use it." He banged it against the side of the dumpster. "Come on. You'd better get out…"

Homeless Hal took that two-by-four and started wailing away.

After a while, the guy stopped resisting. Stopped moving completely.

Homeless Hall grabbed the guy by the ankles. Dragged him outside, and looked at him under the street lights…

"Oh my god! It's Old Scratch Nickels." Hal's eyes widened. "They're going to think I killed him on purpose. They're going to put me in the electric chair and fry me for sure!"

It wasn't too far down the hill to the bridge over the river…

Homeless Hal dragged Old Scratch Nickels down to the bridge. That man was heavy. Hal had leaned Scratch up against a pylon and was catching his breath when he heard footsteps coming.

He took off, ran back to the dumpster, climbed inside, shut the door, lay down, pulled a piece of cardboard over himself, set his watch alarm to wake him up before trash pickup, and slept very soundly.

Now, jogging along the sidewalk on her way home from a late night run was Midnight Mary. She wasn't a lady of the evening. They called her Midnight Mary because she was a society woman who loved to exercise after dark.

She was minding her own business, trotting across the bridge when she saw this fellow sprawled out with his feet sticking out across the whole sidewalk. How rude was that? I'm trying to have a nice pleasant evening run and this fellow is blocking the whole path.

"Sir," she said. "Sir, could you move your feet, please? Sir? Please move your feet…"

There was no answer. He didn't move.

"I've got pepper spray," she warned.

"I've got a stun gun. I've got a derringer."

He still didn't move.

She darted closer and hit him in the face with the pepper spray. She shot him with the stun gun. She fired twice with the derringer.

Then she realized what she had done.

"Oh my goodness." She stepped closer and stared at the man's face. "It's Old Scratch Nickels. They're going to think I killed him on purpose. They're going to put me in the electric chair. They're going to fry me for sure!"

It wasn't too far from the sidewalk to the edge of the bridge, where he could be pushed into the water. She dragged and pushed him over there. He was heavy! She had his feet over the side and was just about to push him over when a siren sounded.

A police car pulled up.

She took off. She ran home faster than she had ever in her life, took a shower, washed herself off with lava soap, scrubbed herself with a loofa, dried herself off, threw the towels and clothes into the wash, crawled into bed, and slept very soundly, although she did not jog after dark ever again.

Pulling up in that patrol car was Honest Juan Williams, the most trustworthy and uncorruptable police officer on the force. He shined the light over and spoke through his microphone.

"Sir, move away from the edge. Sir? Sir, there is no problem so severe that a visit with a psychiatrist or a social worker can't help. Sir?"

Honest Juan Williams got out of the car, left the door open so it didn't slam and startle the man. He walked over slowly and calmly in a non-threatening manner. He put a kind and gentle hand on the man's shoulder and watched in horror as Old Scratch Nickels fell off the bridge and tumbled into the water below.

"Oh my gosh! It's Old Scratch Nickels." Honest Juan had a lot of enemies. "They're going to think I killed him on purpose. They're going to put me in the electric chair. They're going to fry me for sure!"

Honest Juan Williams panicked and did the only dishonest thing of his entire career—he fled the scene of the crime. He ran back to his squad car, slammed the door, shifted into gear, drove full speed up the hill—and smashed into the side of a station wagon full of escaping bank robbers.

He arrested the robbers, he got interviewed on TV, got a reward, he went home, and he slept quite soundly.

Downstream, in the early morning sunrise was Digger Dan.

Digger Dan was out in the Bay with his bull rake collecting clams. He had his waders on. He was pulling up the clams when all of a sudden something big hit him in the legs. Whomp!

He didn't think twice. He took his bull rake and started wailing away at it…

It stopped moving. He reached down and lifted it up.

Water dripped off the flaccid chubby face.

"Oh my god," Digger Dan sighed. "It's Old Scratch Nickels."

He shook his head. "They're going to think I killed him on purpose."

He spat. "They're going to put me in the electric chair and fry me for sure."

But Digger Dan had other skills

besides clamming.

He was a trained taxidermist.

He towed Old Scratch Nickels and floated him into shore. He dragged him up the beach and loaded him into the back of his truck.

He took him to his workshop. He worked fast. He emptied him out, filled him up with sawdust and sewed up all the holes.

Dan loaded Old Scratch Nickels back into the pickup. Drove downtown, right to City Hall. Put him on a hand truck and brought him up the service elevator to the third floor. Put him behind his desk.

Put a cup of coffee right next to him.

Dan went home. Slept very soundly.

That morning the secretaries were shocked to find Old Scratch Nickels already at his desk.

And from that day on he was the first one in. He was the last to leave. He worked evenings and weekends.

He stopped taking bribes.

He was reelected again and again.

And he is serving to this very day.

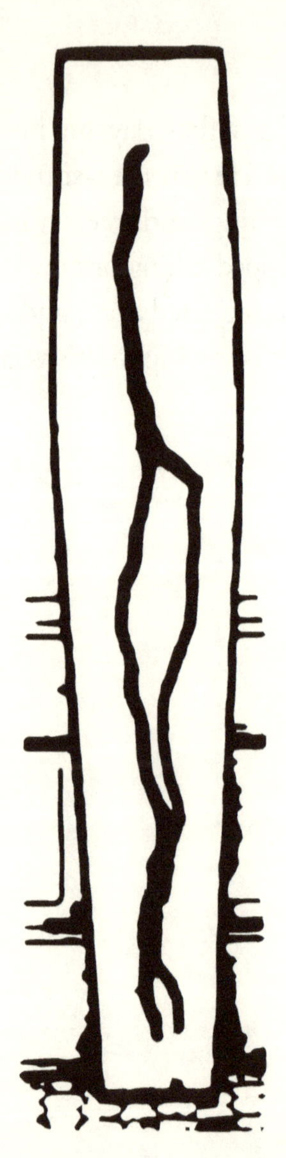

The Old One

stolen from the locked archive at
The Providence Athenaeum

The Narragansett Indians called it "Clths Slaaag," which Rhode Island's founder Roger Williams translated as "The Old One."

Williams joked about it in his journal:

"After a sparse meal of fish and corn, Canonicus, the Sachem, warned me not to build my home on the Eastern hill. He said that was where 'The Old One,' a horrific monster, lived and fed. His vivid description reminded me of the demonic stories told by Popish priests to cow the superstitious. Most probably a rabid bear."

Williams was wrong. Seventeen years later, his second son, Elijah mysteriously vanished and was discovered three days later at the mouth of a cave concealed by a fallen apple tree. The boy's hair and skin had turned white. Three fingers on his left hand were gone, as if they had been gnawed off. Elijah had lost his mind and never spoke again.

Roger Williams' heart was broken. He spent much of the rest of his life abroad in England.

In 1860 when his bones were dug from the family plot to be reinterred beneath his statue in Prospect Park, the popular story was that an apple tree had eaten through his corpse, and the roots had taken the shape of his leg bones. The truth was much darker.

In his diary, Stephen Randall, a

witness wrote, "The stench that emitted from the opened grave was beyond imagining. There lay Roger Williams, looking as well preserved as the day he was interred. Yet his eyes were open, his mouth peeled back baring his teeth in a rictus of horror. When Elder Brown bent down to close the poor man's eyes, the body disintegrated into thousands of wriggling worms. Those who were present fled, and when we returned all that remained were the roots of the apple tree, looking strangely like a leg bone."

Moses Brown discovered the mangled corpse of a slave girl in the basement of his East Side home in 1773. No one knew who she was or how she had died,

Brown wrote, "The corpse's condition was appalling. Her back was scarred with lines that John said betrayed the excessive use of a lash, but reminded me of both the jagged tares rendered by an animal's claw and the infected ruin of a child caught in a wave of jellyfish tentacles."

A short time later, Moses Brown freed his slaves and began working for abolition.

Edgar Allen Poe, the author, was the next to write of the thing that lived beneath the Hill. In the margin of the original manuscript for the famous poem, "The Raven," Poe wrote in a crabbed hand, "Only in the form of a black bird I can indicate the monstrosity. I have tried again and again to describe the Old One, but language fails me, and the words I use seem unnatural and unreal." Following his failed courtship of Sarah Helen Power (Whitman), Poe spent weeks wandering up and down

Benefit Street in a laudanum-induced haze. Many say that he never recovered.

The most direct references to the creature came from Howard Phillips Lovecraft, who is still famous for his horrific tales of the Necronomicon and "The Great Old Ones" with unpronounceable names. Lovecraft lived most of his life on Providence's East Side, at the tip of a triangle between the land near where Elijah Williams was discovered, and the basement of Moses's Brown's house.

"…that cellar in our childhood house was my constant nightmare," Lovecraft wrote to his brother Peter near the end of his life. "While you and Emily laughed and played, I peered into the darkness. I fear that soul-destroying blackness corrupted me somehow."

More recently, 1983, a party thrown

by a group of Rhode Island School of Design Students in an abandoned train tunnel ended in horror. The Providence Journal reported that "After the tear gas and pepper spray cleared, police found thirteen naked students, their backs bleeding as if they had been struck with a whip. One girl was dead. Police have no suspects, but report the probability of drug abuse."

In 2003, when more than 30 house cats were reported missing, the newspaper attributed the disappearances to a coyote roaming the neighborhood, yet suggested that "small pets and children remain inside after dark."

An article in an alternative broadsheet, *The Agenda,* suggested in 2006 that the changing landscape of the City was bringing the horror to the surface. "The rivers have been uncovered, a highway is shifting, and a billion dollar project has dug underground sewage overflow tanks beneath the hills where Roger Williams once planted his crops. What else have the construction crews dug up?"

Shortly afterwards, the sidewalk behind the First Baptist Church in America on Benefit Street caved in and disintegrated.

Week after week, at WaterFire in Providence bonfires are lit in the river and haunting music is played while tens of thousands of people wander through the smoke as an ancient ceremony is reborn and recreated.

Less than six months ago, the mutilated body of a Brown University student was found on a hills in the North Burial ground. The details were hushed up, photographs of her corpse were deleted and television cameras were kept far from the scene.

When asked to comment about the rumors of the Old One, the Mayor refused to answer. "This was clearly the work of a sick human being. We have far more pressing problems in this city in terms of education and infrastructure. Don't bother me about this nonsense."

Have the rising of the seas, the building of roads and moving of earth disturbed the creature? Are the bonfires and music and the crowds drawing the monster closer, bringing it nearer and nearer to the surface?

This isn't something that you can discover safely in the warm glow of a cell phone search. It is hard to tell with all the noise.

But if you listen carefully, as you wander the darkened streets of Providence late at night, perhaps you will hear a sound, a soft and slurping sound, as if a moistened finger was caressing the cartilage next to your ear.

If you hear this sound, do not stop. Do not turn around. Do not scream. It feeds on fear and despair.

Enjoy your breath. It may be your last.

About the Author

Mark Binder holds a Masters in English and Theater from the Trinity Rep Conservatory. He is a graduate of Columbia University, where he studied storytelling with Spalding Gray and mythology with T.E. Gaster and David Damrosch. An award-winning recording artist and live performance storyteller, he relishes spinning tales for multigenerational listeners around the world. He is the author of more than two-dozen books and audio books. Mark lives in Providence with his wife and family.

If you enjoyed this, you will also enjoy the audiobook and the companion:
What Cheer!

To purchase a copy and for information about tour dates, visit
markbinderbooks.com/shop